THE CANTALOUPE CAT

Author's dedication: For my Mother, for believing in this book, for my loving husband Fred, with thanks for his skillful editing, for our sons, our cats, and for Jerry, the original cantaloupe cat.
Illustrator's dedication: To Mom, for gentle pushes, David, Kate, and Laura, for their love and support, and in memory of my Dad.

Published by:
Hannacroix Creek Books, Inc.
1127 High Ridge Road, #110
Stamford, CT 06905
Phone (203) 321-8674 Fax (203) 968-0193
E-mail: hannacroix@aol.com   On the Internet: www.hannacroix.com

Printed by Friesens Corporation in Canada.

Library of Congress Catalog Card Number: 98-73266

Yager, Jan, 1948-
The cantaloupe cat / written by Jan Yager ;
illustrated by Mitzi Lyman. -- 1st ed.
p. cm.
SUMMARY: Like Jerry, the cat who likes to eat cantaloupe, every animal and every person is special and unique in some way.
Includes bibliographical references.
ISBN: 1-889262-12-9

1. Cats--Juvenile literature. 2. Individuality--Juvenile literature. 3. Self-esteem--Juvenile literature. I. Lyman, Mitzi. II. Title.

PZ10.3.Y34Ca 1998   [E]
QBI98-959

THE CANTALOUPE CAT

Written by Jan Yager
Illustrated by Mitzi Lyman

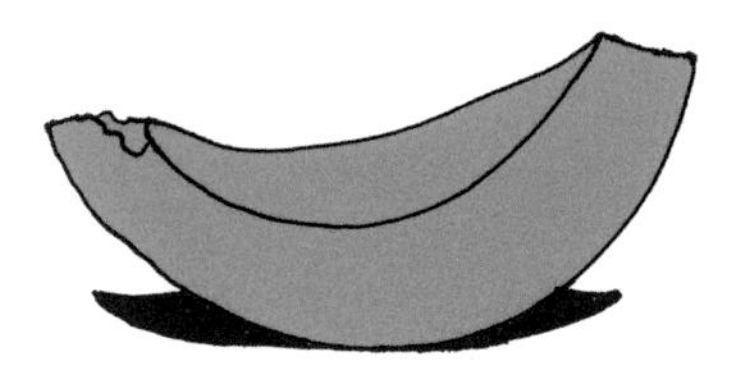

HANNACROIX CREEK BOOKS
STAMFORD, CT

While other cats
Chase pieces of rope,
Jerry stands in the kitchen
Eating cantaloupe.

While most cats
Go to a bowl for a drink

Jerry gets his water
Out of the sink.

All cats like pats,
And playing with socks,

But Jerry enjoys spending
His time in a box.

Some cats, as you may know,
Like to go outside.

Not Jerry. He's an indoor cat.
His home is his castle
And he guards it with pride.

Sometimes all day,
In the window he'll sit

All by himself or
With his sister Bridget.

Some cats play with dogs
And other animals too.

Do you have a friend
Who likes to play with you?

Jerry's my pet
And he's special you see,
Special like you

Special like me.

JAN YAGER is an author, teacher, and speaker who has worked as an assistant editor in the School Division of Macmillan Publishing Company. She has a Ph.D. in Sociology from the City University of New York and lives in Stamford, Connecticut with her husband, two sons, and two cats. The author of 12 nonfiction and fiction adult titles, this is her first children's book.

MITZI LYMAN, a graphic designer and artist, has a B.S. in Human Development from the University of Massachusetts. She has studied painting and illustration at the Arts Students League and The School of Visual Arts in New York as well as at the Corcoran School in Washington, D.C. She lives in Westport, Connecticut with her husband, two daughters, and two dogs. This is her first children's book.

Suggested Questions for Discussion

In the story, what is special about Jerry? Now tell me what is special about you?
Draw a picture showing something that is special about you.
Do you have a pet? What kind of pet do you have? Tell me what's special about your pet?
Do you have a brother, or a sister, or a cousin? What is special about your brother or sister or cousin?

Related Children's Books

Addabbo, Carole. Illustrated by Valentine. *Dina the Deaf Dinosaur*. Stamford, CT: Hannacroix Creek, 1998.
Meddaugh, Susan. *Martha Speaks*. Boston: Houghton Mifflin Company, 1992.
Morris, Ann and Elizabeth Falconer. *My Cat Peter*. New York: Simon & Schuster, 1986.
Sutton, Eve, illustrated by Lynley Dodd. *My Cat Likes to Hide In Boxes*. NY: Scholastic,, 1973.
Walley, Dean. Illustrated by Merrily Johnson. *The Book of Me!* Kansas City, MI: Hallmark Cards, Inc., N.D.
Wheeler, Cindy. *Bookstore Cat*. NY: Random House, Inc., 1994.
White, Nancy. Illustrated by Gioia Fiammenghi. *Why Do Cats Do That?* NY: Scholastic Inc., 1997.